Invitations! Invitations! Join our

Springtime
Celebrations

Story and Illustrations **Mojgan Roohani**

Rhyming Verses **Viva Tomlin**

This book has come out of many years of collaboration with my close friend Viva, working with children to hold their celebrations. My thanks can not be adequately expressed for her endless patience and gift to capture my vision and feelings with such attention to nuances of language and historic detail, and in rhyme!

This book is especially dedicated to Mary Nura, my granddaughter, who is growing up, like so many children in the world, with diverse cultures and Faiths.

First published 2023 English by CreateSpace
for Amazon www.amazon.com
ISBN: 9798375259345

The rabbit and the flowers, in this story,
help us enjoy visiting together
some springtime celebrations.

It is a special time of year
But rabbit's feeling lonely here!

So many friends are out to play!
But she feels shy! What should she say?

She waves. They soon play happily.

"We love new friendships," all agree.

"It's spring! Each has a festival.

I'd love to celebrate them all!"

"We love new friendships," all agree.

"It's spring! Each has a festival.
I'd love to celebrate them all!"

"Now is the time for visiting!
I should have something I can bring."

Sweet little rabbit thinks, then hops,
And filled with happy thoughts, she stops.

"FLOWERS!" That is the best, she's sure.
She sniffs and likes it even more!

Somehow some garden flowers
have grown

From seeds the warm spring breeze
has blown!

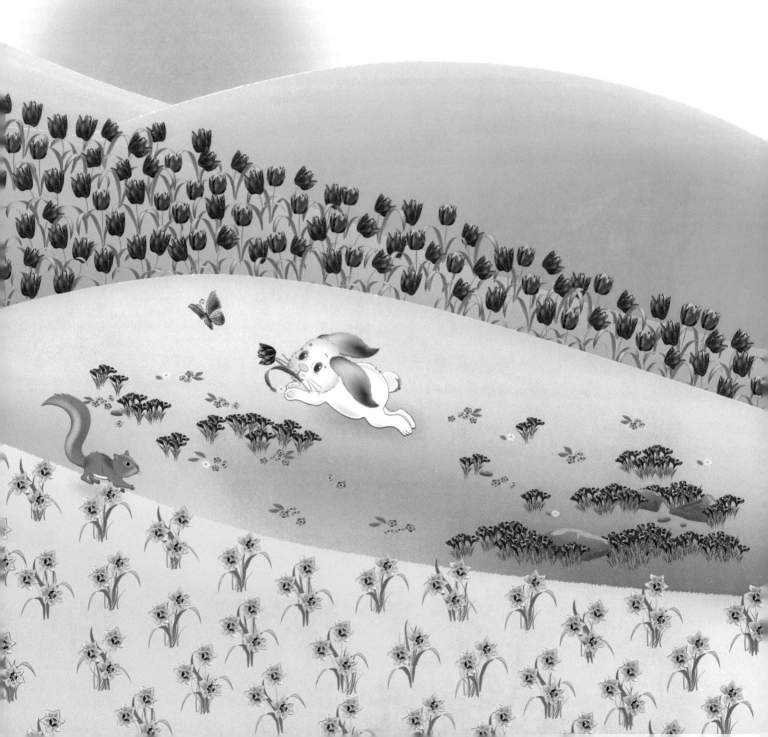

"So beautiful! Red, purple, blue,

And even yellow flowers too!"

She hops with joy to add a pink.
"This makes a lovely bunch, I think!"

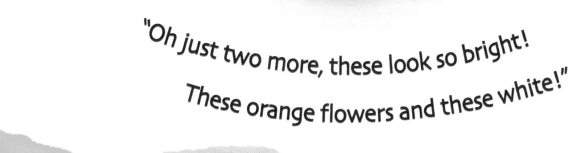

"Oh just two more, these look so bright!
These orange flowers and these white!"

"But now what can I do? I fear
I just keep dropping them! Oh dear"

"How sweet! My lovely flowers, I see
You have arranged yourselves for me!"

"I'm HAPPY for the invitations!
Let's go now to the celebrations!"

Visits and gifts of love will be
A joy for friends and family.

With fun and laughter, we show fear
Of scary things will disappear!

Rainbow faces, clothes and hair,

Showering blessings everywhere!

Tulips, hyacinths, apples, fishes . . .
Joyful feasts and New Year wishes!

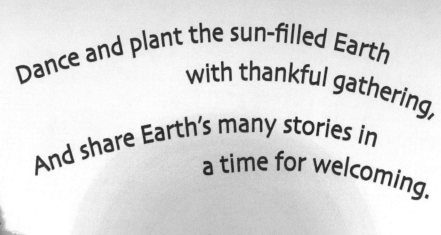

Dance and plant the sun-filled Earth
with thankful gathering,
And share Earth's many stories in
a time for welcoming.

This Festival calls to the earth,
"All peoples should be free!"
Our matza shared, our story told
with friends and family.

Songs of praise and sweet surprises
Lighten our hearts as the sun rises.

So lovely the moon-rise,
    so pure like our hearts,
As Ramadan ends and
    our special Feast starts!

HAPPY

Lotus flowers and lanterns bright,
Glow with thoughts of peace this night.

"We are the flowers of one garden ..." come and see

Ayyám-i-Há
Bahá'í (Bahá'u'lláh)

A time when the days before the last month of the year, a month for the Fast and purity, are set aside for gifts and for sharing our unlimited bounties and blessings with others.

Spring Equinox
Indigenous peoples (of the Americas and all the world)

A time to remember and value how human beings are interconnected with all living things, must live together in harmony and renew the promise to the Earth to take care of it.

Purim
Jewish (Story of Queen Esther)

A joyful costume party in celebration of the time when Queen Esther saved the Jews from the evil minister.

Naw Rúz or Nowruz
Zoroastrian (Zoroaster)
Bahá'í (The Báb and Bahá'u'lláh)

A New Year celebration for Persians of all Faiths, including Jewish, Zoroastrian, Christian, Muslim and Bahá'í, also a Holy Day for Bahá'ís around the world at the end of their Fast.

Holi
Hindu (Krishna)

A springtime celebration of the power of love and of good over evil, full of the colors of the flowers.

"It makes happy neighborhoods wherever we may be."

Wesak or Vesak
Buddhist (Gautama Buddha)

The celebration of the birth, enlightenment and passing of the Lord Buddha, filled with light, purity and peace.

Eid al-Fitr Sometimes falls in Spring
Muslim (Muhammad)

Celebrating the breaking of the month-long Fast of Ramadan, Muslims aim to become closer to their loved ones and grow spiritually. They do this by fasting for purity.

Easter
Christian (Jesus the Christ)

A joyful celebration of the power of light, new life and hope to raise up humankind.

Passover
Jewish (Moses)

It celebrates the right to freedom for all peoples of the world, by remembering the emancipation from slavery.

Riḍván
Bahá'í (Bahá'u'lláh)

A twelve-day Festival first held in a beautiful garden full of roses and nightingales, celebrating that Bahá'u'lláh fulfills an ancient promise of a new spiritual Springtime of the glory of World Peace, in unity of all people and life on earth.

Game Time

Look at each picture on the hills
Then find which Springtime Celebration
each picture comes from in the story.

Made in the USA
Las Vegas, NV
29 February 2024

86478761R00029